Rose and the Delicious Secret

BOOK 3

Fairy Blossoms

Rose and the Delicious Secret

By Suzanne Williams
Illustrated by Fiona Sansom

■ HARPERTROPHY®
AN IMPRINT OF HARPERCOLLINS*PUBLISHERS*

Fairy Blossoms #3: Rose and the Delicious Secret
Text copyright © 2008 by Suzanne Williams
Illustrations copyright © 2008 by Fiona Sansom

Library of Congress Cataloging-in-Publication Data is available.
ISBN 978-0-06-113939-0

Typography by Andrea Vandergrift
❖
First Edition

Contents

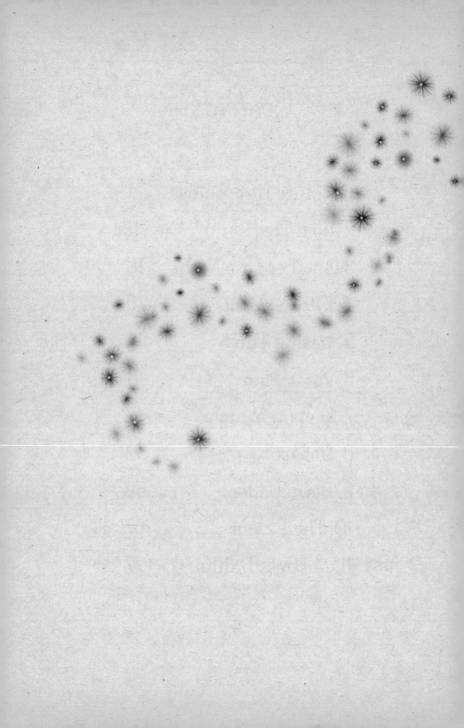

1

Strange Happenings

Dinner was over, but Rose and Marigold hadn't yet left the table. Sipping raspberry tea from a snail-shell cup, Rose began to look over her wish-granting notes.

Marigold pushed her plate aside. "Want to study together?" she asked. The fairies' first exams at Mistress Lily's Fairy School were in only two days.

"I'd better study alone," Rose replied. She didn't want to hurt Marigold's feelings; but if the two of them worked together, she was sure they would wind up talking more than studying.

"Well, okay then." Marigold slid off her satin-covered toadstool. She fluttered her wings. They were decorated with yellow and orange swirls—a perfect match with the yellow silk gown and orange sash she was wearing. "See you later."

"'Bye," said Rose. Flipping over a page of notes, she sighed. No one studied as hard as she did. Why, she'd barely spoken

to any of her friends in the last few days—
including Marigold. And besides reviewing
for exams, she was still working on her ball
gown.

Rose rubbed her tired eyes. She'd stayed up
late the last two nights, practicing invisibility.
Yet she still had trouble making herself
vanish completely. There was always an elbow
or a fingertip left visible, glowing faintly
green.

Mistress Lily had *tried* to help. "You need
to relax more," she'd said. But Rose only knew
how to work hard. She'd never been good at
relaxing. So far she hadn't been able to stay
invisible for more than a few seconds at a
time. None of the other fairies seemed to be
having as much trouble. Violet, of course, was
already an expert. But that was because she'd
learned from her grandmother before coming
to school at Cloverleaf Cottage.

Clink! Rose glanced up. Bink had begun to clear dishes from the table. A type of fairy called a brownie, he was taller than Rose. Not much taller, though—and flower fairies are barely two inches tall!

"Sorry I'm so slow to leave," said Rose.

"What?" Bink jumped, sending a fistful of forks clattering to the floor. He hadn't even noticed she was still there.

Rose leaped up to help pick up the mess.

"I prefer to do it myself," Bink said grumpily.

Rose sat. She'd forgotten how much brownies hated to have anyone do their work. Still, it wasn't like Bink to be so gruff. "Is something the matter?" she asked. "You're pricklier than a pinecone."

"Don't mind me," Bink said. "It's probably nothing." He brushed back a lock of reddish brown hair that had fallen over one eye.

"Done with your tea yet?" he asked politely.

Rose handed him her not-quite-empty cup. Then she gathered up her notes and started to rise from her toadstool.

Bink sighed. "Of course, if you *really* want to hear about it . . ."

Rose sank back down. It was on the tip of her tongue to say that she needed to study. But after all, she *had* asked. "So, what's going on?"

"It started five days ago," said Bink. "I was late for work one morning and—"

"Overslept, I bet," Rose interrupted with a smile. It was no secret that Bink didn't like getting up early.

He frowned but went on. "My first morning task is to churn the milk into butter. But when I arrived, my work had already been done. The butter was cooling in the icebox."

"Maybe Cook did it," said Rose.

Bink's eyes widened. "He'd *never* offend me like that. Besides, he lives in the village. He comes in early, but not early enough to do *my* chores. Anyway, he commented that the butter was richer and creamier than usual. He wondered what I'd done to make it turn out better."

"Ouch," said Rose. "That must have hurt."

Bink nodded. "And the next morning was the same—only there was bread dough rising on the counter too."

"You make bread?" asked Rose.

"No, Cook makes it. And when the loaves came out lighter and tastier than ever, he yelled at me. He thought that I'd done *his* job!"

Rose tapped her fingers together, thinking. "Who else works in the kitchen?"

"No one," said Bink. "It's only Cook and me." He paused. "Cook threw a fit this morning when he discovered a tray of frosted hazelnut cookies sitting on the counter. He accused me of getting up in the middle of the night to bake them! He would have thrown them out if I hadn't stopped him."

"Were those the cookies you served for lunch today?" asked Rose.

"Yes," said Bink. "Why?"

"Just wondering." No way was Rose going to tell him how delicious the cookies had been. Since coming to Cloverleaf Cottage, she'd missed the talents of the hobgoblin baker who worked for her family. But the cookies at lunch today had tasted every bit as good as his. Marigold, who was somewhat plump, had even claimed to "love, *love*, LOVE!" them. Three *love*s was high praise—

even for Marigold.

Bink looked around the room and then lowered his voice. "Shall I tell you what I think is going on?"

"What?" asked Rose.

"Someone is playing a trick on Cook and me."

"Maybe," Rose said. "But who could it be?"

"Who indeed?" said Bink. "It must be someone who lives here."

"I suppose so. But besides the junior fairies and you, there's only Mistress Lily."

Bink nodded. "We can safely count Mistress Lily out, so . . ."

"Surely you don't suspect any of us fairies!" Rose protested.

Bink shrugged. "What else can I think?"

Rose opened her mouth to defend her friends. Then she closed it again. Though she didn't want to admit it, she was certain Bink was right. Someone at the cottage had to be doing this. But which of the junior fairies would play such a trick?

2

Up a Tree

Bink stacked the dishes. "I'd better get back to work."

"And I've got to study," said Rose. "May I investigate? I might be able to discover who the secret baker is."

Bink nodded. "Thanks, Rose." He picked up the stack of dishes and hurried to the kitchen.

Rose grabbed her notes, then flew off in

search of Daisy and Poppy. She found them sitting on the lowest branch of the huge oak tree that grew behind Cloverleaf Cottage. Daisy was studying, but Poppy was reading a book.

Rose hovered near them, her wings fluttering. "Mind if I join you?"

"Not at all," said Daisy. She scooted over to make room.

Rose sat down between the two fairies. As quickly as she could, she described her conversation with Bink. When she'd finished, Poppy asked, "So, who do *you* think is sneaking into the kitchen at night—or in the wee hours of the morning?"

Rose shrugged. "I haven't a clue."

Daisy tugged at one of her curly blond ponytails. "I can't imagine any of us doing that."

"I'm not so sure," said Poppy. "The triplets

did get into mischief the first week of class."

"Yes," said Rose. "But Heather, Hyacinth, and Holly are baby crazy, not *food* crazy. The only one of us who's really crazy about food is . . ."

"Marigold!" finished Daisy. "But does she know how to cook?"

"I know she used to fix meals with her

family," Rose said reluctantly. "But that doesn't mean anything."

"Maybe yes and maybe no," Poppy said. "I say we keep an eye on her—*and* on the others."

"Okay," Daisy agreed. "But I bet whoever is doing this doesn't realize she's hurting Bink's feelings and making trouble between him and Cook. She probably thinks she's being helpful."

Rose nodded. "Maybe we should just tell everyone what's been going on. If the secret baker knew she was upsetting Bink and Cook, she'd stop, right?"

"Probably," Poppy said. "But then we'd never find out who the culprit was!"

Daisy blinked. "If I were the one doing this, I'd be embarrassed to have everyone know. Wouldn't you?"

Poppy raised an eyebrow. "*Is* it you?"

14

"Ha-ha," said Daisy. "I can't even boil water. If I could, I'd still probably spill it."

The fairies giggled. Daisy was a bit of a klutz.

"I'll talk to Marigold," said Rose. "Could the two of you speak with Violet and the triplets?"

"Sure," said Poppy.

Rose wondered if Poppy honestly thought Marigold was the secret baker. Wouldn't Marigold have told Rose if she were helping out in the kitchen? After all, they were best friends! But then again, she and Marigold hadn't talked a lot lately.

"Are you ready for exams?" Daisy asked, changing the subject. "I can't believe they're in just two more days. And we have to turn in our gowns tomorrow!"

Rose groaned. "My seams are still uneven. And I have to study more. I was hoping I wouldn't have to stay up late again tonight. But there's so much to do!"

Poppy rolled her eyes. "Puh-lease, Rose. You and Marigold are tops at dressmaking. And you're the best student in class!"

"Do you really think so?" Rose asked. "No matter how hard I try, I still can't get the hang of making myself invisible."

"Sounds like you're trying *too* hard," said Poppy. "Don't think about it so much. Just do it."

"Thanks for the advice," said Rose. Mistress Lily had said something similar, of course. "See you later."

As she fluttered down from the tree, Rose thought about Poppy's shape-shifting ability. Poppy was half pixie, and pixies could transform into all sorts of things—beetles and mushrooms, for instance. She could have disguised herself—perhaps as a mouse—to sneak into the kitchen at night. Rose sucked in her breath. What if Poppy had only cast suspicion on Marigold to keep Rose from suspecting *her* as the secret baker?

3

Another Late Night

But it was ridiculous to think that Poppy could be the secret baker, thought Rose. Poppy and Daisy were Bink's best friends. They wouldn't want to do something that would upset him—not deliberately, anyway. Still, Rose decided, she would keep an eye on everyone, *including* Poppy and Daisy.

Rose flew to her flower bed. The junior

fairies all slept in a garden beside the cottage. Rose sank into the soft petals of a pink rose. She would study for an hour, then fly up to the classroom to finish her dress. After that, she would practice invisibility. That was what she *planned* to do, anyway. But her bed was so comfy, and she was so tired. Her eyelids grew heavier and heavier. Finally Rose's study notes slipped out of her hands and she fell asleep.

She awoke with a start in the middle of the night. Scolding herself for falling asleep, Rose threw off the petals that covered her like a blanket. Invisibility practice would have to wait, but at least she could finish her dress. On her way to the cottage, she flew past the yellow marigold where Marigold slept. She was curled up on top, fast asleep.

As she breathed in and out, Marigold's wings fluttered gently. They were dark blue tonight and decorated with silver moons to match her pajamas. Rose smiled. She couldn't picture her friend rising early each morning to churn butter and bake bread.

Once inside the cottage, Rose flew over the balcony to the classroom. Her gown's seams would have seemed straight enough to anyone else, but Rose wanted them to be perfect. When she finished with that, she changed the cloth-covered buttons up the back of the gown to pearl. Finally, she stood back to admire her work.

The white satin dress sparkled with tiny diamonds. The sleeves were puffy, but not *too* puffy; and the skirt had layers of ruffles. *Perfect*, thought Rose. She hoped Mistress

Lily would think so too.

Yawning, Rose tucked her wand away. As she flew out of the cottage and headed toward bed, she glanced down at Marigold's flower. Rose was startled to see that her friend was gone. A moment later, Rose heard the cottage door open and close, and soon Marigold appeared. Flapping her wings slowly, she drifted toward Rose.

"What are you doing up at this hour?" Rose asked. Marigold couldn't have been to the classroom. Rose would have seen her.

Marigold didn't answer.

Rose tried again. "Why were you inside the cottage?"

Ignoring her, Marigold floated down to her flower bed and closed her eyes.

Rose gave up. She could talk to Marigold in the morning. But as Rose settled onto her own flower bed, she wondered if Marigold had been in the kitchen. What if her friend was the secret baker after all? Too tired to think more about it, Rose waved her silver wand that sparkled with rubies and changed her gown into a pink nightie. Sinking deep into the center of her rose, she was soon asleep.

She awoke just before dawn. Her flower was swaying back and forth, as if pushed by a strong wind. Rose peeked over the side of her bed and was surprised to see the earth move. Then she heard muffled footsteps. They sounded like they were coming from underground. But that was crazy! A few moments later, the swaying stopped, the footsteps faded away, and Rose fell asleep again.

The next time Rose awoke, Marigold was

hovering over her. "Hurry up, sleepyhead. You've missed breakfast, and class starts in five minutes!"

Rose sat up. "Why didn't you wake me?" she asked, rubbing her eyes.

Marigold shrugged. "I figured you must need the rest. Here." She handed her a blackberry scone. "I saved this for you."

"Thanks," said Rose. She was confused. Marigold was acting like she didn't even remember what had happened last night!

Rose took a bite of the scone. "Mmm," she said. "This is *delicious*."

"Isn't it?" Marigold smiled. "I ate three of them.

Rose brushed the crumbs from her nightie. She wanted to tell Marigold she'd seen her last night. She wanted to ask if Marigold was the secret baker. But there was no time for that now. Waving her wand, she changed her nightie into a dark pink dress with a lacy collar and sleeves. Then she and Marigold flew off to class.

4

Kitchen Visits

Mistress Lily smiled at the eight junior fairies as they took their seats. She usually dressed in blue, but today she was wearing a red gown belted at the waist with a wide satin ribbon. Rose thought the dress looked fabulous.

"I've been looking over your gowns this morning, and they're all quite wonderful," the teacher said.

Rose breathed a sigh of relief. Not that she'd *really* thought Mistress Lily wouldn't like her dress.

The teacher tucked a strand of long, golden hair behind one ear. "Your exams are tomorrow afternoon, of course. And I've decided to cancel classes today to give you extra time to study."

A grateful murmur ran through the room.

"After lunch I'll post your dressmaking grades on my office door," said Mistress Lily. "You may come up to check them then."

As soon as they were excused, the junior fairies flew down from the balcony. Rose and Marigold landed together on the main floor. "I sure am glad for the extra study time," said Marigold. "I just can't seem to get all those wish-granting rules to stick in my head."

As they left the cottage, Rose changed

the subject. "Did you know that strange things have been happening in the kitchen lately?"

Marigold's face turned red. "Really?" she squeaked. "What kind of things?"

Was Marigold feeling guilty? Rose watched her carefully as she told her all about the secret baker.

"Well, that explains a lot," Marigold said when Rose had finished speaking. "Bink practically glared at me when I asked him to give Cook my compliments on the scones this morning. I wonder if he thought that *I* was the secret baker!"

"Why would he think that?" Rose asked. She hadn't yet mentioned seeing Marigold out of bed last night. She was anxious to hear her friend's reply.

Marigold gave her a wide-eyed stare.

"How would I know?"

The two fairies were standing on the lawn in front of the cottage. At the foot of the lawn was a crystal-clear stream. Poppy waved to them from the jeweled bridge that crossed over the stream. "Hey, Rose!" she called out. "I need to talk to you."

"Excuse me, please," Rose said to Marigold.

"Sure," said Marigold. "See you at lunch."

Rose fluttered down to the bridge. "How come you weren't at breakfast this morning?" Poppy asked her right away.

"I was up late last night and slept in," said Rose.

Poppy gave her a suspicious look.

"Hold on," Rose said. "*I'm* not the secret baker." But why shouldn't Poppy suspect her? After all, Rose had suspected *her,* too!

"Daisy talked to Violet," Poppy said now.

"Violet told her something interesting. Several nights ago she woke up early. She was hungry, so she flew to the cottage to get a snack. And guess what? She saw Marigold fly out of the kitchen!"

Rose's stomach sank. Before she could comment, Poppy went on.

"That's not all. Two nights ago Heather saw Marigold fly out of the cottage—at *midnight*."

"I saw her, too," Rose said with a sigh, "last night."

Poppy frowned. "Did you ask if she was the secret baker?"

Rose shook her head. She had been about to ask, but Poppy had interrupted their conversation. "If Marigold *is* the secret baker," she said, "she'll stop now, right? Now that she knows she's upsetting Bink and Cook."

"I suppose," said Poppy.

Rose smiled uncertainly. "Problem solved, then." But was it? It seemed like Marigold *must* be the secret baker. But perhaps there was some other explanation for her puzzling behavior. And if so, Rose wanted to know what it was.

5

Wishes Three

Bink served huckleberry cake for lunch. "I'm sure *yours* would be better," he said with a scowl as he handed Marigold her plate.

Marigold flushed pink. "What are you talking about?"

"*You* know," said Bink. "You were seen!"

"What do you mean?" asked Marigold.

Rose felt sorry for her friend. Marigold

seemed genuinely confused. Someone must have told Bink about her late-night kitchen visits. Unless he had seen her himself.

"I'm not the secret baker, if that's what you think!" Marigold exclaimed.

"Really?" Bink sounded like he didn't

believe her. "Then why have you been sneaking into the kitchen at night?"

Marigold blinked. "I was in the kitchen?" She sighed. "I'm afraid it's happening again, then. I must have been sleepwalking."

Everyone stared at her.

"Sleepwalking?" asked Poppy.

"Well, sleep-*flying*, actually. I used to do it a lot when I was younger. Now it only happens when I'm worried about something—like our exams."

No wonder Marigold hadn't answered her last night, Rose thought. Though Marigold's eyes had been open, she had been asleep!

Bink frowned. "Were you sleep-*baking*, too?"

Marigold laughed. "I don't think so. But I might have been sleep-*snacking*. I found crumbs in my flower bed this morning."

"But if you're not the secret baker, who is?" asked Bink.

"Good question," Rose said. Just the same, she was glad it wasn't Marigold.

The triplets had left the table early. Now Holly called down from the balcony, "Mistress Lily just posted our dressmaking grades!"

The fairies leaped from their toadstools to flutter up to the classroom. Rose, however, turned back for a moment. "Don't worry, Bink," she said. "I have a plan for catching the secret baker red-handed—or *flour*-handed, anyway. I'll talk to you about it later, okay?"

For the first time in days, Bink smiled back. "Okay."

Rose's heart beat fast as she zipped over the balcony. Had she really done her best job on her gown?

The fairies were crowded around a piece

of paper tacked to the office door. "Look, Rose!" Marigold squealed excitedly. "You and I tied for the highest grade!"

Rose scanned the list. All of the fairies had done well. No one had gotten lower than a B. But she and Marigold were the only two fairies with A-pluses.

Rose beamed. Yet as pleased as she was with her dressmaking grade, there were still

two tests to take tomorrow afternoon. The invisibility test worried her the most. So when Marigold asked if they could study together for the wish-granting exam, she hesitated.

"*Puh-lease*," Marigold pleaded. "I'm really nervous about it."

"All right," Rose said at last. She would just have to practice invisibility later.

Marigold hugged Rose. "Thanks!"

The two fairies sat on the lawn to study. Marigold had trouble remembering the answers even to simple questions—like how many wishes humans could have—so Rose made up some rhymes to help her. "I see wishes three," she chanted in a singsong voice. "Try it."

"I see wishes three," Marigold sang. "Hey, I think this will help!"

Rose made up some more rhymes for

Marigold, but teaching them took a long time. She'd have to practice invisibility after dinner. Of course, practice hadn't helped much so far. But what else could she do?

6

Rose's Plan

Bink's shoulders were slumped as he served dinner that night. And while he waited for the fairies to finish, he looked down at the floor and sighed a lot.

"You and Cook are still fighting, aren't you?" Rose said. She'd heard them arguing in the kitchen earlier that evening.

Bink nodded gloomily. "Cook still thinks

I'm the secret baker. He thinks I'm after his job!"

"That's ridiculous," said Poppy. "You would never do that."

"Yes," said Bink. "But if I can't uncover the *real* secret baker soon, I'm afraid I'll lose my job. Cook threatened to fire me!"

Daisy gasped. "He can't do that, can he? Mistress Lily wouldn't allow it!"

Bink shook his head sadly. "Mistress Lily may run the school, but *Cook* runs the kitchen."

"You could still look after the ponies," said Poppy. That was also Bink's job.

"Yes," said Bink. "But I *like* working in the kitchen, too."

Rose was the last to finish eating. As she was about to leave the table, Bink stopped her. "Will you help me? You said you had a plan."

"I did, didn't I?" said Rose. How could

she have forgotten? "Here's my plan: We hide in the kitchen late tonight and keep watch." It was a good thing exams weren't until tomorrow afternoon. She could sleep in.

"I thought about that myself," said Bink, "but I'm a heavy sleeper. I was afraid I might fall asleep and then wouldn't wake up if someone came."

"We'll take turns keeping watch," said Rose. "I bet Marigold, Poppy, and Daisy will want to come too," she added. With five of them on the job, there was no way the secret baker could slip past! "Shall we meet in the kitchen at midnight?"

"Sounds great," said Bink. "Thanks a lot, Rose!"

"You're welcome," she replied.

Later, Rose found her friends out on the lawn, studying. She told them her plan and they all agreed to help. Afterward, she flew to a quiet corner of the cottage to practice her invisibility.

Mistress Lily had said they'd have three tries to cast a successful spell. Nothing could show—not even the tip of a shoe. And the spell had to last for one full minute!

Rose practiced and practiced in front of a mirror. Over and over she waved her wand and shouted, "Conceal!" Then she would hold her breath and watch herself vanish. More often than not the edge of her dress or the top of her head still showed, glowing green. And no matter how tightly she gritted her teeth, the spell wouldn't hold. All too soon she would reappear in a burst of gold glitter.

Feeling close to tears, Rose collapsed onto a bench. Her wand arm felt so wobbly, she couldn't hold it up any longer. Hard work had never failed her before. Why was

invisibility so difficult for her when it came so easily to others? Mistress Lily had told her to relax more. And Poppy had said, "Don't think about it so much." But so far the advice hadn't helped. How could she *not* think about getting the spell just right?

Rose rubbed her eyes. She was so tired. But in less than an hour it would be midnight. Then she would join her friends to watch for the secret baker.

7

Keeping Watch

"Let's keep watch in teams," Rose said. She and her friends had hidden under a table in a corner of the kitchen. "Marigold and I can take the first watch."

Bink sat up straight. "So will I."

"Okay," said Poppy. "But wake Daisy and me if anything happens."

"All right," said Rose.

Poppy and Daisy curled up on a woven rug on the tile floor. Soon they were fast asleep.

The kitchen seemed spooky in the dark. Moonlight shone through the window and glinted off three sharp knives lying on the counter. Rose tried not to look at them. Instead, she focused on glowing embers in

the fireplace and listened to the soft *tick tock* of the clock above the sink.

After what seemed like hours (but was really only a few minutes), Rose began to feel sleepy. It didn't help that Bink and Marigold kept yawning. Finally, Bink's chin dropped to his chest, and he began to snore softly. "Wake up," Rose whispered. She gently shook his shoulder.

Bink snuffled a little, but went on sleeping. "Never mind," Marigold said. "We can keep watch without him." To stay awake, the two fairies whispered to each other. After a while, however, they both fell silent and drifted off to sleep.

Rose was startled awake when Marigold stirred beside her. Still snoring, Bink had fallen onto his side. Rose glanced at the clock. It was one thirty. In another half hour it would be Daisy and Poppy's turn to take over the watch. Rose thought about waking Marigold but decided to let her go on sleeping.

Listening to the *tick tock* of the clock, Rose began to nod off again. Then the floor beneath her started to shake, and she heard faint clomping sounds. *Footsteps!* And just like the night before, they sounded as if they were coming from underground! The footsteps grew louder. But before Rose could wake the others, the sounds stopped. Then, as if pushed from below, a square tile in front of the table began to rise.

Rose gasped. Whoever was under the floor would see her and her friends! With no time to think, she grabbed her wand from her pocket and waved it over everyone. "Conceal!" she hissed. She felt a tiny tingle as the spell took effect, cloaking them all in invisibility. Not a speck of green light shone through.

"Huh?" said Poppy, rubbing her eyes.

"Sh," Rose warned. She pointed to the raised tile.

Poppy's eyes widened. With a finger to her lips, she quietly woke the others.

The five friends stared as the tile was shoved to one side. Moments later, a little man pushed himself up onto the kitchen floor.

8

Hobart

The little man wore a pair of red trousers, a tattered blue jacket, and pointy-toed shoes. He was taller than the fairies but shorter than Bink. After dropping the tile back into place, he warmed himself by the fire, then scurried over to the icebox. He grabbed a pitcher of cream from inside and emptied it into the butter churn.

He pushed the handle up and down, his
arms pumping faster than a hummingbird's
wings. Then the little man began to sing:

"*Hobart the Hobgoblin,*
that is my name.
Though I churn and I knead,

I don't do it for fame.
To me it is only
a funny little game.
I let other creatures
take all the acclaim."

"Or the *blame*," whispered Bink.

Rose had been so interested in watching Hobart, she'd hardly thought about her invisibility spell. Without realizing it, she'd held the spell for much longer than a minute. But now Hobart paused as if he'd heard Bink speak, and looked around. Instantly Rose's wand hand tensed, and her invisibility spell gave out.

Dropping the churn handle, Hobart stared at the fairies. Rose fluttered toward him. "Don't be afraid," she said. "We just want to talk to you."

But Hobart let out a frightened squeal and raced out of the kitchen. "Stop! Come back!" yelled Bink. The fairies took off after the hobgoblin. He tore through the cottage and out the front door. The fairies followed him outside but soon lost sight of him.

Rose put her ear to the ground, listening. Sure enough, she could just make out the faint clatter of footsteps below. "He's underneath us," she said.

"An underground tunnel!" Bink exclaimed. "Dwarves built mines in this area long ago."

Rose wondered if Mistress Lily knew about the tunnels.

"Do you think Hobart's been down there long?" asked Daisy.

"At least a week," said Bink. "That's how long the secret baking has been going on."

"He can't be very comfortable living in an

old mine tunnel," said Marigold.

"I agree," said Rose. "Let's find him. We'll convince him to live somewhere else. Then he won't cause any more problems." She paused. "That's what you want, Bink, right?"

"Uh . . . right," said Bink. But he didn't sound sure.

"We can reach the tunnel through the entrance in the kitchen," said Poppy.

The fairies ran back into the cottage. But when they tried to lift the tile in the kitchen floor, it wouldn't budge. "There must be other entrances," said Daisy. "Hobart found one outside. We'll just have to search."

Rose snapped her fingers. "I bet there's an entrance in the garden!" She explained about hearing footsteps under her bed the night before. "Until now, I thought I'd only imagined them."

The fairies searched near their flower beds and all around the outside of the cottage. But after an hour they still hadn't found another entrance. Rose peered at the base of the giant oak that sheltered the cottage. How good it would feel to lean back against the trunk and rest. It was crazy to keep searching—especially with exams that very afternoon!

Suddenly she noticed a thin slit in the bark of the trunk. Holding her glowing wand in front of her, she examined the cut more closely. With growing excitement, she saw that it formed an arched doorway. Was this a tunnel entrance? And if so, would it open?

Rose shot colored sparks from the tip of her wand to signal to her friends that she'd found something. Then she pushed against

the door with all her might. To her surprise,
the door swung in easily—too easily, in fact.
Rose fell through the door and slid down the
tunnel, which sloped like a slide.

9

Down Under

When the tunnel leveled out, Rose finally stopped sliding. She raised her glowing wand to look around. The tunnel's rocky sides were thick and gray. Ahead of her it curved to the right and began to slope downward again.

"Rose?" Marigold's voice echoed along the tunnel. "Are you in here?"

"Yes!" Rose called back.

In a moment, her friends caught up to her. "Brr," said Poppy. "I'm cold." Her breath came out in little white puffs.

"Let's keep going," said Rose. "Hobart is down here somewhere."

Bink took long strides to keep up with the fairies as they flew. The deeper into the tunnel they went, the colder the air grew. Soon everyone was shivering. "This is s-s-silly," Rose said through chattering teeth. "We d-don't have to be cold!" Her fingers were icy stiff as she waved her wand. "Fringe and frippery, frocks and frills," she chanted. There was a burst of glitter, and suddenly she was wearing a fuzzy, hooded pink jacket and pink fleece mittens.

The other fairies pulled out their wands too. Soon everyone was warmly dressed, including Bink. "I hope it's not too puffy," Daisy said, looking at the thick red jacket she'd made for him.

"Not at all," said Bink. "It's terrific." But in fact, the jacket made him look like a big, round tomato.

They kept going. Before long they reached a spot where the tunnel split into two tunnels. "Which way should we go?" asked Marigold.

"Good question," said Rose. She wished she had a good answer. They peered down each passage. But even with glowing wands, it was impossible to see very far.

Rose frowned. "I guess we'll just have to pick one and see where it leads."

The first tunnel came to a dead end within a few minutes. The group backtracked and took the second tunnel. After a while, it opened up into a wide, sandy chamber. "Look!" Bink exclaimed. "Footprints!"

Pointing their glowing wands toward the ground, the fairies flew in for a closer look. Sure enough, a set of pointy-toed footprints led across the floor.

"Those must be Hobart's!" Poppy exclaimed.

Rose nodded. "Let's follow them."

The footprints stopped outside a big wooden door that was open a tiny crack. Soft sniffling noises came from the other side. It sounded like Hobart was crying!

Rose held a finger to her lips. She peered through the crack into the dim room and could just make out a figure tying up a bundle of clothes. The figure was singing a sad little song:

"Hobart the Hobgoblin
is leaving today.
I liked being here,
but now I can't stay.
Nobody wants me.
I'm just in the way."

At that moment, Daisy's wand slipped out of her hand. "Oops," she said as it hit the door and clattered to the ground.

Hobart stopped singing. In a shaky voice he called out, "Is someone there?"

Bink picked up Daisy's wand. Pushing the door wider, he stepped into the room. The fairies fluttered in behind him.

"Bright!" Hobart cried, shielding his eyes from the glowing light of the wands.

Bink cleared his throat. "See here," he said gruffly. "You've caused a lot of trouble these last few days."

"I didn't mean to," said Hobart. "Honest."

"It's true that you're a good baker," said Bink. "But—"

"I *love* your hazelnut cookies!" interrupted Marigold. "And your blackberry scones are so light and fluffy and . . ." Her voice trailed off as Rose nudged her.

"Thanks," Hobart said. "The scones are my own special recipe."

"That's nice," said Bink. "But the point is—"

"And your butter is wonderful, too," Daisy interrupted.

"Yes," Poppy agreed. "How do you make it so creamy and . . . ow!" she yelped. Rose had tugged hard on one of her wings.

"Let's let Bink finish," Rose said sweetly.

"Listen, Hobart," said Bink. "Your secret baking has made things difficult between Cook and me. It's hard when someone takes over your work and—"

"I understand." Hobart hung his head. "I was just leaving."

"Wait," said Bink. "I wasn't finished yet." He shifted his feet. "It's hard when someone takes over your work and . . . does a better job of it." He shrugged. "It's true. Your butter *is* the best. And so is your baking. If you really want to stay, we can try to convince Cook to give you a job."

Hobart hopped right over his bundle and hugged Bink. "Thank you!" he exclaimed. "I promise you won't regret it!"

Rose smiled at Bink. She'd always known he had a big heart.

10

The Exams

Hobart led everyone back through the tunnel. "I *love* kitchens," he said happily. "They're toasty-oasty warm." At the tunnel's end, he pushed up on the square tile in the kitchen floor, and everyone climbed out.

Cook was already at work, frosting a freshly made buttermilk spice cake. He was so startled to see everyone that he frosted his thumb. "Where did you . . . Who is . . . What's going on?" he stammered.

"We found your secret baker," Rose told Cook.

Hobart clasped his hat to his chest. "Hello," he said shyly.

"A *hobgoblin*?" Cook asked.

"That's right," said Poppy. "He was living in an old mine tunnel."

Cook frowned at Hobart. "Do you know how much trouble you've caused?"

Hobart stared at the floor.

"He didn't mean to cause trouble," said Marigold. "He just likes to cook."

"And the kitchen is warm compared to his cold little room," added Daisy.

Rose smiled at Cook. "I bet you could use some extra help."

"Humph," Cook said. "Bink and I manage just fine on our own."

"Sure," Bink agreed. "But we *do* have a lot of work. If Hobart did our early-morning jobs, we could both get an extra hour of sleep."

Poppy grinned. "With more sleep, maybe you two wouldn't be so short-tempered all the time."

Cook glared at Poppy. "*I'm* not short-tempered!"

"Neither am I!" growled Bink.

The fairies laughed.

Bink turned red. "I see what you mean."

Cook blushed too. "I've never liked getting up early," he admitted. He looked at Hobart. "My grandmother was part hobgoblin. She was the best bread maker in the village. Her cinnamon rolls were heavenly."

"I make cinnamon rolls, too," said Hobart. "But they're probably not as good as your grandmother's."

"Your blackberry scones were delicious," said Cook. "How do you make them so light?"

Soon the two of them were deep in a discussion about their favorite recipes.

Bink and the fairies quietly left the kitchen. The fairies flew outside to their flower beds to grab a few hours' sleep before lunch and their afternoon tests.

During lunch, Violet and the triplets were excited to learn about Hobart, but they were sorry to have missed an adventure. "At least you got a full night's sleep!" Poppy said.

When it was time for the exams, all eight fairies flew up to the balcony. "Good luck," said Marigold.

"Same to you," Rose said, and she and Marigold took their seats.

The wish-granting test was fill-in-the-blank. Rose got stuck on a couple of questions, but then she remembered the little rhymes she'd taught Marigold. *When you help someone else, you often help yourself,* she thought. She was sure Bink would agree. Now Hobart had a job, and Bink would get an extra hour of sleep every morning!

When Marigold turned in her test paper, she smiled and gave Rose a thumbs-up. "Thanks to you, I just may have passed," she whispered.

In spite of her successful spell last night, Rose was still a bit nervous about the invisibility exam. *Just relax,* she reminded herself. Like Poppy had said, the trick was not to think about it too much. You just had to let it happen. And if some small part of her showed, or she couldn't hold the spell for a full minute, at least she would have tried her best.

When it was Rose's turn to become invisible, she breathed deeply a few times. Then she closed her eyes and thought about how she had felt in the kitchen last night.

Opening her eyes again, Rose smiled. She could *do* this! With a steady hand, she waved her wand. "Conceal!" she commanded.

Rose felt a tiny tingle and looked down. Not a single part of her glowed green. Keeping her hand steady, Rose relaxed. The spell was so much easier to hold on to when she didn't tense up. Practice and effort helped one learn, she thought, but it was also important to

let go of worries about doing things exactly right.

When Mistress Lily announced that one minute was up, Rose knew she could hold the spell longer. But she lowered her wand. In a burst of gold glitter, she became visible again.

"Very good, Rose," said Mistress Lily. She sounded pleased. But then she added, "Come see me in my office after everyone's been tested."

Am I in trouble? Rose wondered. Maybe she hadn't done well on her wish-granting exam after all. Then she had another thought. Mistress Lily must have found out about Hobart. What if she was angry that Rose and her friends had gone looking for him? After all, it was Rose's idea. If anyone had gotten lost or hurt, it would have been all her fault!

Rose took her seat. She clasped her tiny hands together to keep them from trembling and waited for the testing to end.

11

Mistress Dahlia

Rose's wings fluttered nervously as she knocked on Mistress Lily's door.

"Come in," her teacher called. "Have a seat," she added pleasantly.

Rose glanced around the room as she sat down. The last time she'd been here, the office had been a real mess. Magazines and papers had covered the desk and floor. Mistress Lily

77

had been away for a while and the substitute teacher, Mistress Petunia, wasn't particularly neat.

The office was tidy now. A bouquet of forget-me-nots sat in a thimble vase on the edge of Mistress Lily's desk. Above the desk hung a portrait of a striking and intelligent-looking fairy. Had the portrait been there before? Rose couldn't remember. She studied the fairy in the picture. Something about her looked familiar, but Rose was sure they had never met.

Mistress Lily was watching Rose. "I wonder if you know who that is?" she asked.

Rose shook her head. "A former teacher here?" she guessed. She couldn't think why else the portrait would be hanging in Mistress Lily's office—unless the fairy was a relative of hers.

"Good guess," said Mistress Lily. "You're

absolutely right. Mistress Dahlia was the *founder* of Cloverleaf Cottage." She looked at Rose curiously. "Have you really never heard of her?"

"I don't think so," Rose said. "Should I have? She *does* look kind of familiar. But if she founded the school, she must be ancient."

Mistress Lily laughed. "Perhaps not *that* old. But I'm surprised you've never heard of her. She happens to be your great-great-aunt."

"Really?" No wonder the fairy in the portrait looked familiar! "I don't know much about my relatives," Rose admitted.

"A lot of us don't. I just thought you might have heard of her because of her connection to the school."

"How did *you* know she was my great-great-aunt?" Rose asked.

"I saw a family resemblance the first time I met you," Mistress Lily replied. "I did some checking of Mistress Dahlia's family tree, and out popped your mother's name—and yours."

"Wow!" said Rose. She couldn't wait to tell the other junior fairies. "Was that the only reason you wanted to see me?" she asked hopefully. "To tell me about my famous aunt?"

"Actually, no," said Mistress Lily. She clasped her hands together on top of her desk. "I met Hobart this morning."

Rose gulped. Was she about to be scolded?

"I feel I may have let you down," said Mistress Lily.

"Why?" asked Rose. This was not at all what she'd expected!

Mistress Lily sighed. "The safety of all who live and work at Cloverleaf Cottage is my responsibility. I knew about the mine tunnels, but I thought that they had all been properly sealed. I should have checked."

"But how were you to know that Hobart had found a way in?" Rose protested.

"I should have been more aware of what

was going on," said Mistress Lily. "But I didn't even know there was a problem in the kitchen."

"That's not your fault," said Rose. "Somebody should've told you."

"True," said Mistress Lily. She looked straight at Rose. "I wonder why no one did?"

Rose blushed. "I guess *I* should've told you," she admitted. After all, she *was* the oldest of the junior fairies, if only by a couple of months.

"Of course, Bink or Cook might have said something too," said Mistress Lily. "Or any of the other junior fairies." She smiled at Rose. "You *will* let me know—in the future— if anything seems amiss? I want to keep the cottage a safe place for all." She paused. "Your classmates see you as a leader, you know. And so do I."

"Thank you," said Rose, pleased with the compliment. "But what about Hobart? Can he stay?"

Mistress Lily nodded. "Cook fixed him a bed in a little room off the kitchen."

That sounded much better than living in a cold, dark tunnel. Rose was sure Hobart would be quite comfortable there.

"By the way," said Mistress Lily. "Congratulations on your exams. You got the highest score in class!"

"Really?" Rose had almost forgotten about the tests!

"Really," said Mistress Lily. "I think Mistress Dahlia would be very proud of you."

Rose felt warm all over. "Thanks." She left Mistress Lily's office, feeling happier than she had in days. She was pleased to have done well in her studies—and excited to find out about her famous great-great-aunt. But she was even happier that Mistress Lily saw her as a *leader* and thought that the other junior fairies did too.

Thinking of Hobart, Rose decided to make up her *own* rhyme:

> *"My name is Rose,*
> *as everyone knows.*
> *Where there's a need,*
> *I'll step in to lead.*
> *My friends will help too,*
> *because that's what friends do."*

Then Rose flew downstairs to join Marigold and the rest of her fairy friends.

Whimsical adventures await at Mistress Lily's Fairy School!

Suzanne Williams
Fairy Blossoms 1

Suzanne Williams
Fairy Blossoms 2
Poppy and the Vanishing Fairy

...usy and the Magic Less...

Suzanne Williams
Fairy Blossoms 3
Rose and the Delicious Secret